The Monkeys and the Water Monster

and two more monkey stories

The Monkeys and

he Water Monster

and two more monkey stories

The Monkey and the Crocodile

The Stolen Necklace

Retold by BERNICE CHARDIET
Pictures by RAINEY BENNETT

SCHOLASTIC BOOK SERVICES
NEW YORK · TORONTO · LONDON · AUCKLAND · SYDNEY · TOKYO

To B. de R.

These three stories are based on material in *The Jataka or Stories of the Buddha's Former Births,* translated from the Pali by various hands under the editorship of Professor Edward Byler Cowell, Cambridge University Press, 1898.

13 12 11 10 9 8 7 6 5 4   6 7 8 9/7 0/8

Printed in the U.S.A.

The Monkeys
and the
Water Monster

Once upon a time there was a terrible monster with a bright blue belly and eyes as red as fire and long, sharp claws and a face as white as chalk.

The monster lived in a thick, wild forest. He hid at the bottom of a lake where no one could see him. And he gobbled up everyone who came into the water to drink.

One day, many monkeys came to live in the forest. They came with their king, who was very wise. The king called all the monkeys to a meeting.

"My friends," he said, "this forest is not safe. A water monster lives here in one of the lakes. He hides at the bottom where no one can see him. And he gobbles up everyone who goes into the water.

"You must ask me first before you go into a lake. You must ask me first before you drink any water."

The monkeys agreed to do just as the wise king said.

A few days later, some of the monkeys went deep into the forest. They saw a beautiful lake. The lake looked calm and peaceful. The water sparkled in the sunlight.

"Let us go in and drink," said one of the monkeys.

"No, no!" said the others. "We must wait for our king. We must ask him first before we go into the lake."

So the monkeys sat down in the reeds near the shore. And they waited for their king to come.

They waited and waited. They got very, very thirsty. But they did not go into the water.

At last, the monkey-king came swinging through the trees. "You must be very thirsty," he said to the monkeys.

"Yes," said the monkeys. "But we did not go into the lake to drink. We waited to ask you first."

"Quite right!" said the king. "We must find out if the lake is safe."

Then the monkey-king began to walk
around the lake. He looked very carefully
at the ground. He saw the footprints of some
deer going down to the water.

A little further on, he saw the footprints of a tiger going down to the water. He saw the footprints of a jackal, and the footprints of elephants and lions and rabbits. All the footprints were going down to the water.

The monkey-king went back to the monkeys. "My friends," he said, "let me tell you what I found."

I found many footprints around the lake.
I followed every track.
But all of the footprints went DOWN
TO the water.
Not one single footprint came back!

"Do you know what this means?" asked the king.

"No," said the monkeys. "What does it mean?"

"It means all these animals went into the water to drink *and never came out again.* Do you know why?" asked the king.

"No, why?" said the monkeys.

"Because," said the king, "the monster is HERE! He is hiding in this lake!"

The monster heard what the monkey-king said. He got so angry, he rose right up from the water.

"Do not listen to him!" the monster shouted at the monkeys. "This lake is safe. Go in and drink at once!"

"But aren't you the water monster?" asked the monkey-king.

"YES, I AM!" the monster shouted.

"Then how could the lake be safe?" said the king. "Won't you eat us if we go in?"

"YES!" roared the monster. "I will eat the whole lot of you."

"Then we will not go in," the monkey-king said.

"Oh, no?" the monster shouted. "Well, I'll get you just the same. I can hide at the bottom of any lake — any lake in this forest. You will have to go in, or you will never drink water. You will never drink water again!"

"Oh, yes, we will!" the monkey-king said.
"We will drink from this very lake."

"Good!" said the monster. "Go ahead,
then! I'll be waiting for you." And he went
back under the water.

The monkey-king turned to the monkeys and said, "Do not be afraid. We will find a way to drink *without* going into the water!"

The king picked up one of the reeds that grew around the lake. "Now do as I do," he told all the monkeys. And he blew into the reed to make it hollow.

Each and every monkey picked up a reed. And they blew into the reeds to make them hollow.

Then the king put one end of his hollow reed into the water.

Each and every monkey did the same.

"Now drink!" said the monkey-king. And all the monkeys drank. They sipped up the water through the hollow reeds. They did not have to go into the lake.

The water monster could not get one single monkey, not even one monkey for his dinner!

And from that day to this, the reeds that
grow around that lake are hollow. You can
see for yourself, if you ever pass that way.

The Monkey
and the Crocodile

Once upon a time, long, long ago, a monkey lived high up in the trees along a river.

One day, a crocodile and his wife came swimming by.

The crocodile's wife could see the monkey jumping through the treetops.

"Ah! The King of the Monkeys!" she thought. "I must have his heart to eat." So she said to her husband, "You must catch that monkey — by hook or by crook! You must catch that monkey and bring me his heart."

The next day the crocodile waited for the monkey to come down to the river to drink. Then the crocodile called out:

Ho, there! Monkey!
How would you like a treat?
How would you like some mango fruits
That are sweet and ripe to eat?

"I would like that very much," the monkey said. "Where can I get some?"

"Right across the river," the crocodile said.

"But how will I get across?" said the monkey. "I do not know how to swim."

"I will take you on my back," said the crocodile.

The monkey hopped on the crocodile's back. "Thank you," he said. "You are very kind."

"Not at all!" said the crocodile. And he

began to swim. But when he got to the middle of the river, he stopped. "I am going to drown you, Monkey!" he said.

"Drown me?" shouted the monkey. "Why are you going to drown me?"

"My wife wants to eat your heart," the crocodile said.

"Is that all?" The monkey laughed. "Your wife wants my heart? Why didn't you say so? I would have brought it with me."

"What?" said the crocodile. "You do not have your heart with you? How could that be? Isn't it in your body?"

"Of course not!" said the monkey. "We monkeys hang our hearts in trees."

"I do not believe that," the crocodile said. "I am going to drown you!"

"Wait!" the monkey shouted. "I can prove

I am telling the truth." And he pointed to one of the fig trees that grew along the river. "Look! You can see for yourself."

The crocodile looked at the fig tree. Sure enough! The rows of figs looked like rows of hearts hanging from the branches.

"*Hmmm! So the monkey is telling the truth*," the crocodile thought. "Which heart is yours?" he asked.

"You cannot see it from here," the clever monkey said. "Take me to the tree and I will give it to you."

So the crocodile turned around and took the monkey to the shore.

In a wink, the monkey jumped off the crocodile's back.

In a wink, he climbed the fig tree and called:

Crocodile, Crocodile,
Hear me speak.
Your back may be strong,
But your mind is weak.

"Did you really think I kept my heart in a tree? Ha! Ha! Take *this*! It's all you'll get!" the monkey shouted. And he threw a fig down to the crocodile.

Then the crocodile knew that he had been tricked. And he swore to get even with the monkey.

The next day, the crocodile came back. But the monkey was gone! The crocodile went looking for him up and down the river.

At last, the crocodile came to a place where the river got very narrow. And there he saw the monkey coming down from his tree.

The crocodile hid under the water and watched.

The monkey came down to the shore of the river. He jumped to a rock that was sticking out of the water. Then he jumped from the rock to a little island where mango trees were growing.

As soon as the monkey's back was turned, the crocodile lay down on top of the rock.

He did not move.

He did not make a sound.

He lay very, very still and waited. "This time," he thought, "that monkey will not get away from me."

All day long, the monkey stayed on the island. He ate the sweet, ripe mangoes to his heart's content. By the time he was ready to go home, it was almost dark.

29

The monkey ran down to the water. He looked at the rock and got ready to jump. But, suddenly, he stopped. "Something is wrong with the rock," he thought. "SOMETHING IS ON IT! Could it be...? Is it...? It looks like — THE CROCODILE!

"So he's trying to trick me again," the monkey thought. "Hmmm! We'll see about that."

Then the clever monkey called out, "HELLO, ROCK!" There was no answer.

The monkey called again. "HELLO ROCK, IS THAT YOU?" Still no answer.

"What is the matter, Friend Rock?" called the monkey. "Why don't you answer me the way you always do?"

"*Oh!*" thought the stupid crocodile. "*So the rock and the monkey are friends.*

30

"Go ahead and answer!" he whispered to the rock. But the rock kept quiet.

"Well, if you won't answer," the crocodile whispered, "I will have to answer for you." And he called out, "HO, THERE! MONKEY!"

"So, it IS you, Crocodile — just as I thought," said the monkey.

"Yes, it is," said the crocodile. "And this time you won't get away."

"You are right," the monkey said. "I may as well give up."

"Yes," said the crocodile. "You may as well. You may as well jump right into my mouth."

"Well, then," said the monkey. "Open your mouth and close your eyes. And here I come — with a big surprise!"

The monkey jumped. But he did not jump into the crocodile's mouth. He jumped on the crocodile's back instead. And from there he jumped to the shore. He climbed to the top of his tree and called:

Crocodile, crocodile, hear me speak.
Your back is still strong,
And your mind is still weak.

"Go home and tell your wife she will *never* have my heart for dinner."

Then the crocodile knew the monkey was too smart for him. And he called out in turn:

Oh, Monkey-king! You are much too
smart.
Never again, will I come for your heart.

And after that, he left the monkey alone.

The
Stolen Necklace

One summer day it was very hot in the palace. So the king invited everyone to go down to the lake for a swim.

The queen took off all her jewels before she went into the water.

She took off her crown.

She took off her rings.

She took off her beautiful diamond necklace.

She gave all the jewels to the chamber-maid. "Keep these jewels safe for me," the queen said. And then she went into the lake.

The chambermaid sat down under a tree. She put the jewels in her lap. "I will keep these jewels safe for the queen," she said.

But it was so hot, she began to feel sleepy. She could not keep her eyes open. Soon she fell asleep.

When the chambermaid woke up, the beautiful diamond necklace was gone!

"Help! Help!" the chambermaid shouted. "Catch the thief! Catch the thief! Someone has stolen the queen's diamond necklace!"

At once, there were guards running everywhere. Everyone was shouting, "Catch the thief! Catch the thief!"

Just then, a poor man came walking down the road. He heard all the shouting. He was very scared. He began to run away as fast as he could.

The guards saw him running. "There goes the thief!" they cried. They ran into the road and caught the poor man. They dragged him before the king.

"Did you steal the queen's necklace?"
asked the king.

"No, Your Majesty," the poor man said.

"Then who did?" shouted the king. "Tell
me or I will throw you in jail!"

The poor man was afraid. What could he
do? He pointed to the gardener who was
standing nearby. "Maybe he did it," the poor
man said.

The king asked the gardener, "Did you steal the queen's necklace?"

"No, Your Majesty," the gardener said. "Maybe he did it." And he pointed to the cook.

The king asked the cook, "Did you steal the queen's necklace?"

"No, Your Majesty," the cook said. "Maybe she did it." And he pointed to one of the ladies-in-waiting.

"Enough of this!" the king shouted. "Throw them all in jail."

Then a wise man stepped up. "Your Majesty," he said, "all these people are innocent. None of them took the necklace."

"How do you know?" said the king.

"The guards were at the gate all day," said the wise man. "No one could have gone in or out without being seen. So we know the poor man did not steal the necklace."

"That is true," said the leader of the guards. "Why didn't I think of that?"

"The others were all in the lake," said the wise man. "They were in the lake, swimming with you. So we know that they did not steal the necklace."

"That is true," said the king. "Why didn't
I think of that?"

Then the wise man turned to the
chambermaid. "Did you see anyone take the
necklace?"

"No!" said the chambermaid. "I did not
see anyone take the necklace. I only saw a
monkey asleep in a tree."

"Maybe the monkey is the thief," the
wise man said.

"Maybe," the chambermaid said. "Why
didn't I think of that?"

"But there are hundreds of monkeys in the garden," said the queen. "How will we find the right one?"

"I think I know a way," the wise man said. "First, you must get me necklaces made of glass beads. Get me all the necklaces you can find. Tonight we will hang them from the bushes. In the morning, we will catch the thief."

"But how?" said the king.

"You will see," said the wise man.

That night the wise man hung the glass necklaces on the bushes in the garden. Then he told everyone in the palace to hide behind the bushes and wait.

They waited and waited until it was morning. The monkeys woke up and saw the glass necklaces glittering in the sunlight. At once, they rushed down from the trees. They put on the necklaces.

At last, there was only one necklace left. One of the monkeys did not take a glass necklace. One of the monkeys was still sitting up in her tree. The others danced around her, showing off.

"Look at us!" they shouted. "We look as grand as the queen."

"Why don't you take a necklace?" said one monkey. "Yes," said another monkey. "You look so ugly without one."

Then the monkey in the tree could stand it no longer. "Who wants an old glass necklace?" she said. "I have a real diamond necklace to wear. It is the necklace of a real queen." And she reached into a hole in the tree and pulled out the queen's diamond necklace. She put it around her neck.

"We'll see who's ugly now," she said. Then, slowly and proudly, she came down from the tree.

The wise man took the diamond necklace from the monkey and gave it back to the queen.

"You see," said the wise man, "we have caught the thief." And then he said:

When there is a thief about,
There is no need to run and shout.
Think instead.
Use your head.
And the truth will out!